11/2020

My Lovely-Loving D...

are Princesses.

♡ Grandma
Pat

The Princess without a Crown

For my princesses, Abigail and Claire
—Nicole

For my mum and dad, thank you for
always letting me follow my dreams.
—Heather

ISBN 13: 978-1-4621-3572-1

Published by Sweetwater Books, an imprint of Cedar Fort, Inc.
2373 W. 700 S., Springville, UT 84663
Distributed by Cedar Fort, Inc., www.cedarfort.com

  Library of Congress Control Number: 978-1-4621-3572-1

Cover design and typesetting by Shawnda T. Craig
Cover design © 2019 Cedar Fort, Inc.
Edited by Kaitlin Barwick

Printed in the United States of America

10 9 8 7 6 5 4 3 2 1

Printed on acid-free paper

The Princess without a Crown

Written by **Nicole G. Ellis** • Illustrated by **Heather Burns**

Sweetwater Books • An imprint of Cedar Fort, Inc. • Springville, Utah

Once there lived
a princess,
in a land not far away.
She loved to wear
her sparkly crown
and dance,
and sing, and play.

She stared at her reflection,
and the freckles on her nose.
She was the tallest of them all,
standing on her tippy toes.

She slipped into her flowy dress
and spun, and turned, and twirled.
No one needed to remind her
she was the princess of her world.

The time came
to leave her castle,
for a few hours
every day,
to a world beyond
her kingdom.
She was a
tiny bit afraid.

"Can I please wear my crown?" she asked.
"It's as sparkly as can be.
Once they see me in my pretty crown,
they'll want to play with me."

Her mother shook her head and smiled.
"Leave your crown at home with me.
They'll like you for simply being you.
Just wait and you will see."

"Can I play too?" she bravely asked.
Could they make room for just one more?
"No, sorry," one of the children said.
"This game's only meant for four."

It made her feel so very sad,
More sad than you might think.
Her nose must be too freckly.
Her shoes must be too pink.

In a room so full of children,
she felt so all alone.
Her eyes filled with little tears.
She wanted to go home.

That night, she climbed up on the counter,
sneaking the makeup from the shelf.
She had watched her mom so many times.
She could do it by herself.

She dabbed on the black mascara,
smudging it a tiny bit.
Then took a bright red lipstick
and smeared it on her lips.

She took the pinkest powder,
and a giant fluffy puff,
and made perfect pinky circles.
"Yes, that should be enough."

She looked at her reflection.
Her eyes opened very wide.
She looked just like a little clown,
though she had really tried.

Her mother came into the room.
Her face looked quite surprised.
She quickly got a warm, wet rag
and started with the eyes.

The princess told her mother
what had happened as she cleaned.
"Maybe if I am beautiful,
the kids will notice me."

Her mother smiled warmly.
"I know just how you feel.
I used to feel the same way," she said.
"And sometimes feel it still."

"It doesn't matter if your eyes
are brown, or green, or blue,
or if your lips are red or plain.
Beauty lives inside of you."

"Beauty is not just on your face.
It's in your heart and in your mind.
Beauty means that you are honest
in all you do, and that you're kind."

"You're a princess."
Her mom's eyes twinkled.
"Though others cannot see your crown,
you can make the world
bright with a smile,
and help others feeling down."

The thing that she then realized
is it doesn't take a crown
to have the power to lift someone
who may have fallen down.

Beauty is not, and never will be, something
you put on or that you wear.
It's not how big or small we are.
It's the kindness that we share.

The next morning, she dressed quickly,
smoothed her hair through with a comb.
She slipped on her pink shoes,
and she left her crown at home.

THE
END